Dedicated to my wife Stephanie.
Thank you for being my best friend and for tending to the garden of our daughters' hearts so well.

And to my five beautiful daughters, Sterling, Elle, Sophie, Ruby, and Royal. Daddy is so proud of each of you! There is nothing you could do to cause me to love you any more or less than I do. You are enough. You will always belong. -*Brandon*

To Emerson, Vera & Margo; our little sprouts who are growing strong and wonderfully green. You are loved even more than all the good seeds in the world!
-*Kevin & Kristen*

Letter from the Author

Seeds and Trees is a tale about the power of words. This story is dear to me. It's probably because it is my story. It follows a young prince who grows up giving and gathering seeds (words). He faithfully plants and waters those seeds daily, until they grow to become very powerful trees. Later, with the help of a friend, he is able to cut down and uproot the bad ones and then replant good seeds in their place.

Now, I do not mean to seem presumptuous, but I think it may be your story as well. If you are a parent, a teacher, a therapist, or an advocate that works with children, I encourage you to do the following. Take a moment and do a self-audit. Think back to where your insecurities first started. Think back to when you first began to doubt that you are good enough. Take a moment to think back to when you first doubted whether you belong. What would your life have looked like without ever believing those lies?

Now, look beside you at the child in your care. Take a moment and think what it would be like for he or she to grow up without those same lies governing their belief system. I believe our words can hurt or our words can heal. This is why I wrote Seeds and Trees. It is my sincere hope that the words and the process outlined in this book will encourage the childlike part of each of our hearts to heal. It's my hope that the words and beautiful illustrations will guide you to and through a process that will bring you hope, encouragement, and freedom.

If you are a child reading this book on your own, I hope you come to believe that you are enough, that you are loved, and that you belong. If anyone tells you differently, what they are saying is simply not true.

"Be careful what you water,
for it will surely grow."

Sincerely,

Brandon Walden

Printed in China.

ISBN: 978-1-947165-68-7

www.thetreasuredtree.com
www.thebraveunion.com

SEEDS and TREES

by Brandon Walden

illustrated by
Kristen & Kevin Howdeshell

In the land of the king lived a special young prince,
who loved climbing trees and playing with friends.

He lived in a castle overlooking the sea.
He played in a field with his two kinds of trees.

He carried a satchel slung low on his waist
to contain all the seeds he might want to exchange.

Each seed was a word that someone had spoken.
Each seed was collected, a trinket, a token.

It didn't quite matter from where it had come,
a stranger, a friend, a whisper made up.

He rose every morning to water the seeds
from each of the words he'd already received.

When someone spoke nicely, not anything mean,
they'd hand him a seed whose true essence was green.

But sometimes the seeds would come bringing pain,
seeds of dark color whose trees produced shame.

Several dark seeds grew quickly, then withered.
Others remained to grow slowly, unhindered.

At the end of each day, he'd admire the seeds
and go plant the new ones and play in his trees.

The trunks and the branches of dark trees were laden
with thistles and thorns, causing pain as he scaled them.

Climbing these trunks and these branches was tricky.
Each part of the tree that he grasped was quite prickly.

Each time the prince climbed, he was bruised and was slit.
Yet trees are for climbing, so through pain he'd persist.

But each time he climbed up his trees clothed in green,
he felt safe and healed, as *those* trees weren't mean.

His green trees were strong,
and they welcomed his touch.

Their branches grew fruit
he could eat or could clutch.

He could sit at the base
or climb to the peak.

He could rest in the branches
or play hide and seek.

As years passed, he noticed his
green trees were weakening.

The trunks at the base of the
trees needed strengthening.

Now the soil had hardened
as life was escaping.

Their canopies were covered.
His dark trees had shaded them.

He would plant his green seeds and dark seeds beside.
Then they'd war with each other and try to survive.

His green trees were strongest with plenty of light,
but his dark trees grew stronger in the darkness of night.

They shared the same water and sunlight to grow,
but the dark trees were hiding the fruit that would show.

The green trees caused life, joy, and peace to grow near,
but the dark seeds killed soil and grew trees clothed in fear.

The field the prince planted had started to show
many trees of two kinds and the fruit that had grown.

The fruit fell like seeds to the soil down below,
filled with seeds to be gathered or given to sow

The young prince grew strong and became a young man.
He continued to plant the seeds placed in his hand.

He invited some friends to come play in his trees,
but some liked to play in his trees from dark seeds.

He had one special friend who always spoke true,
her words filled with grace, as good friends always do.

She never spoke harshly and never spoke lies.
She always spoke gently, with loving replies.

She always gave green seeds and never took back.
She never ran out. There was never a lack.

Her satchel was filled to the brim, overflowing
with greens seeds, not dark seeds, each one for the sowing.

She watched the prince till, plant, and water his grove.
She watched, and she waited until asked to go.

One day, the prince said, "Hey friend, come along."
She humbly agreed and began singing a song.

"To the grove, to the grove,
we will look down below,
at the roots in the soil
and the trees that have grown.

We will care for your green trees
and even plant more seeds,
but your dark trees will fall as this new life is sown."

As he walked in his field with his friend by his side,
the young prince took note as his trees came alive.

Green trees swayed now to the sound of the tune,
But the dark trees stood stiff, clenched their fists,
and seemed rude.

After long years of planting and watering seeds,
they'd grown into mighty and powerful trees.

The prince reminisced as he entered the grove.
He thought back to each tree and the seed that was sown.

He admired the beauty the green seeds created,
but noticed at the roots they were sadly ill-fated.

His friend came prepared and brought tools along.
The prince hadn't noticed, but his friend was quite strong.

The tools that she carried were weathered and humble:
a pickaxe, a saw, and an old rusty shovel.

The friend asked the prince to please pick out a tree,
one causing pain that he'd rather not see.

The prince pointed up to one skinny, dark mass.
His friend said, "Watch this!" then she took out her axe.

With one mighty swing, the tree fell to the ground.
Then his friend dug her shovel deep, deep, deeply down.

The root had to die and
be plucked from the dirt.

Then a green seed was
planted and covered
with earth.

The prince then exclaimed,
"Can you cut down
more trees?"

His friend said, "Oh yes,
and I've plenty of seeds."

Many dark roots had tunneled so deep
that it took them a while to dig underneath.

Dark roots wrapped close 'round the green everywhere.
So, the friend showed the prince how to tend them with care.

Her tools came in handy: the axe, saw, and shovel,
and others the friend had brought here to the struggle.

Then came the day when his forest was green.
Not a dark tree was spotted. Not any were mean.

The friend then surprised the grown prince with some gifts,
some tools for his new daily watering shifts.

She instructed the prince not to plant the dark seeds,
but to go to the cliff to cast them out to sea.

The prince held the green seeds and those were all saved,
but he tossed the dark seeds off the cliffs to the waves.

Then he traveled to new fields abounding with trees,
making sure that he packed his old satchel with seeds...

"To the grove, to the grove, we will look down below,
at the roots in the soil and the trees that have grown.

We will care for the green trees and even plant more seeds,
but the dark trees will fall as this new life is sown."

About the Author

Brandon Walden is a husband and father of five beautiful daughters. He and his family live in Northern California. Brandon often says that Seeds and Trees is his story, cleverly disguised as a children's book. Brandon and his wife Stephanie founded The Treasured Tree, LLC to be a platform that would host and create content for the childlike part in all of us. They encourage parents and families through video, music, books, and speaking engagements.

Find out more information about them at www.thetreasuredtree.com

"Be careful what you water, for it will surely grow."

Follow us on Instagram @seedsandtreesbook or @brandonwalden for information about this book and other content.